MISCREATIONS

5 SHORT TALES OF WICKEDNESS & WOE

SEAN COSTELLO

PRAISE FOR SEAN COSTELLO

"Costello knows his way around the mystery/horror genre, and he keeps the action moving and the suspense ratcheted up tight. He is very much a writer to watch . . ."
—Margaret Cannon, *The Globe and Mail*

Sean Costello is a master of the poignancy of everyday living. In *Here After* he tackles a difficult subject with wit and humanity—and a couple of really good scares. It's a father and son story that will touch your heart."
—Susie Moloney, author of *The Dwelling*

"*Eden's Eyes* is the best horror novel I've read since Stephen King's own *Pet Sematary*. A terrific debut."
—*Rave Reviews*

"Sean Costello's *The Cartoonist* is a wonderful blend of horror, psychology, and the power of suggestion that leaves you guessing right up to the very end!"
—*The New Jersey Grapevine*

"Sean Costello is one of the horror genre's brightest new stars. *Captain Quad* will only enhance his position."
—*Other Realms*

ALSO BY SEAN COSTELLO

Supernatural Horror

Eden's Eyes

The Cartoonist

Captain Quad

Thrillers

Finders Keepers

Here After

Squall

Last Call

Sandman

Fiction

Terminal House

Cover art by Juan Padron

Publisher's Note: This is a work of fiction. Names, characters, places, and incidents are a product of the author's imagination. Locales and public names are sometimes used for atmospheric purposes. Any resemblance to actual people, living or dead, or to businesses, companies, events, institutions, or locales is completely coincidental.

Miscreations/Sean Costello – 1st edition (2026)

This collection is dedicated to MaryAnn Harris, one of the purest, most courageous souls I've known.

FOREWORD

I guess I've always been a hobby writer. For a while in the early 90s, when I sold my first three horror novels to Pocket Books, I entertained the fantasy of hanging up my stethoscope and pursuing my fortunes in the publishing industry, following in the footsteps of giants like King and Koontz. But, as with most lofty ambitions, reality intervened and I went back to writing for the simple joy of it.

In the mid 80s, before finding the grit to tackle a novel, I cut my teeth on short stories. I was—and remain—a *huge* Stephen King fan, and learned most of what I know about the craft from careful disection of the man's enormous body of work. Four of the five tales in this collection took their beginnings from that exploration. I came to think of them as comic books without pictures, in the flavor of King's *Creepshow*, kind of tongue-in-cheek, no-holds-barred horror just for the fun of it.

In this brief anthology, *Writer's Block* and *Frigidaire* are the purest expressions of that attitude. *Duggan's Boots* and *The Apology* are more introspective, but I believe they've stood the test of time. *Road Rage* is a more current effort, stemming from a real-life situation, I'm ashamed to admit. Right up until Frank Murray turns right instead of left, that was me on a bad day after a long night on call in the OR. Unlike Frank, I turned left with my tail between my legs and had that egg-and-fruit breakfast instead.

All in all, I hope you have a pleasant stay with this mixed bag of sweethearts and reprobates.

CONTENTS

1

WRITER'S BLOCK

"Aw *shit*."

Darrin Keene hammered the backspace key, tucked a strip of Taperaser over the typo, and struck the error into oblivion. Now he hit the proper key, completing the word. He reread the short paragraph he'd been laboring over for the past half-hour.

The night was a page torn from an arctic explorer's diary, the last page, unfinished, a page left rasping in the wind next to his frozen body. A cutting northerly rattled the panes, howling through the eaves like a starving she-wolf. Snow smothered everything beneath its crippling weight. Beyond the cabin, the ice-sheeted lake creaked and groaned. It was a bleak night, a night through which nothing warm could endure.

"Starving she-wolf," Darrin said, shaking his head at the overkill.

But it *was* that kind of night. Even his weighty verbiage fell short of describing it. It was the dead of February, and the storm beyond the single-pane windows was fierce and unrelenting.

Darrin had rented this isolated cabin in the Kukagami wilderness for exactly that reason. The setting. What better backdrop for an aspiring horror writer to work against? What richer font of inspiration?

But Jesus, he thought, *what a shit-kicker of a storm*. It seemed to distract more than inspire.

He pushed his chair back from the old Underwood and moved to the stone hearth, the fire dwindling to coals now. The wood-frame cabin was poorly insulated and a bitch to heat (*she-bitch* he thought, grinning). He lay a length of birch on the coals and leaned closer, spreading numb fingers as the papery bark crackled into yellow flame.

It was eight o'clock and dark as pitch. Darrin had by now given up hope of Shelley arriving tonight, and his sense of longing, developed over the course of a lonesome week up here, flared like the bark in the fire. He'd spent the past two days thinking of little else but the voluptuous curves and valleys of Shelley's body, spread out hot and willing on the sheepskin rug in front of the fireplace. He could almost see her there now, in the pixie-dance of flames.

Ah, Shelley. Warm, mammoth-breasted Shelley.

The image vanished as another took its place—Shelley stranded and freezing in a broken-down Honda Civic, halfway up that godforsaken road from the highway. He prayed she hadn't ventured out in this hell-hole of a night. And he realized then, in that instant of terrible possibility, he loved Shelley England. It really was more than the out-of-this-world humping. Somewhere along the line, he'd truly begun to love her.

But Shelley was no dummy. She'd never drive on a night like this. She'd grown up in the North, had heard enough of the real-life horror stories to know better.

Darrin stood a while longer, soaking up the warmth of the fire, then returned to the Underwood. From somewhere outside came the mournful cry of a real wolf, and Darrin's hackles bristled. He hit the tab key and began a new paragraph.

But the cold thing, the bloodless creature conceived in some deep and stinking chasm where even God could not see, was unbothered by the storm. The shrieking wind aroused It, beckoned It. It rose from the muck of the lakebed and thrust a twisted claw up through two feet of ice. The winter air instantly froze the water layering Its scales, but Its taloned digits flexed and shed the icy crust like an exoskeleton.

A tortured groan rose from the ice as it fractured once more from beneath. A second limb poked through into the air. And now a third.

Darrin smirked, excited by the dank menace he was creating. He loved monster stories, had since childhood: *Frankenstein*, *The Werewolf*, *The Blob*, countless others. He knew that credible horror tales, things that could actually happen, had a wider appeal, were more marketable. But the monster stories, usually short, he penned for an audience of one: himself. He secured them like treasures in a special section of his filing cabinet, pulling them out when the light was low and the mood macabre. If he ever got famous, he'd assemble them into an anthology: *Miscreations*, by Darrin Keene.

He got up, paced the room, tried to visualize the rancid aberration that had thus far punched three scaly appendages through the ice. How did you come up with a monster someone else hadn't already conceived? Or did it even matter what the mindless flesh-eater looked like, as long as it left a trail of gore?

He moved to the picture window now, overlooking the lake. And as he watched the swirls and spirals of wind-whipped snow, he heard the eerie moan and faint thunder of ice shifting on the lake. It sure as hell was a creepy sound. The lake was huge and deep, dotted here and there with rocky islands. The gale-force winds had blown its surface clean. Now, it looked like a sprawling black hole in the midst of white desert dunes.

Again he returned to the typewriter, sat, reread the few scant lines. Then stared at the keys, his mind a blank. How would this bit of aquatic pestilence look? He couldn't conjure an image. And he believed he knew why. Tonight, right now, he should've been tangled on the sheepskin rug with Shelley the Amazon woman, Shelley the ravenous she-wolf. Humping. Like animals.

Shit.

It was more than that, though. There was still this diffuse worry that maybe she *had* set out to drive up here. If that were the case, she should've arrived hours ago. He couldn't bear the thought of her marooned in this storm. A dull sense of helplessness nagged him. He was totally isolated here, had *chosen* to be isolated, couldn't even pick up one of Ma Bell's little miracles and dial the seven simple digits that would put his mind at ease.

But it was more even than that. It was this freaking blizzard. Giving him the willies. It was so *cold*. He couldn't imagine a place colder, more lifeless and desolate, than the endless sprawl of hills and bush outside this cabin. If a man got lost out there, it was game over. February in Northern Ontario. Absolute-fucking-zero.

Life-forms . . . none.

Except one, he thought, shivering. *Me.*

Now *there* was something to consider. That whoring wind licking down the chimney, trying to snuff out the fire, and the very real possibility he could freeze to death up here.

He hit the tab key.

No ideas.

Then it dawned. He reached into his backpack and pulled out a joint. He'd almost forgotten about this little muther. It had been intended for him and Shelley. She really got off sexually when she was high. Which meant he did, too.

Damn.

He struck a wood match on the side of the typewriter and lit up. A gift from his dad, this old Underwood. Manual. No electricity here anyway. Typing by oil lamp.

Darrin filled his lungs, stifling the urge to cough, then exhaled an aromatic plume of bliss. Pink Kush, the dealer had called it, from Jamaica.

He took another hit, the anxiety already abating.

And outside, the wind squalled.

There was a dreadful crash behind him now and Darrin lurched to his feet, dropping the joint, knocking the press-back chair to the floor in a clatter of wood against wood. He pivoted, bringing his fists up in a defensive reflex.

Snow billowed along the hallway from the front door. Flames crackled in the hearth, thinning as if to extinguish. The storm was in the living room.

Darrin lurched into the hall, chilled to the marrow. For an eager moment, he thought it might be Shelley, arrived after all. But it had only been the wind, driving the door open with all the force of a battering ram. He caught a glimpse of the blue-white hump that was his snow-covered Jeep as he shoved the door tight to its frame. He threw the iron bolt and leaned against the door, looking with a sort of wonder at the dusting of snow in the hallway, diamonds glittering in lamplight.

He was feeling the dope.

He had a sudden, desperate longing for Shelley.

The cabin creaked, wind lashed the pines. For a wild moment, he considered pulling on his parka, digging out the Jeep and taking his chances.

But no, that would be suicide.

He went back to the Underwood.

Even in the harsh blizzard air, It stank of ooze and rot. Its single, misshapen eye found the yellow rectangle of light that was the picture window and was drawn to it. The gob of putrid protoplasm that functioned as Its brain, a malign nerve centre knowing only hunger, propelled the beast forward, up the snow-crusted incline toward that warm yellow spill.

"O*kay*," Darrin said aloud, pleased. He retrieved the fallen joint and relit. "*Now* this sucker's coming to life. Oh mama, I can almost smell It." He filled his lungs and exhaled, filled and exhaled. Already he could feel the weed heightening his imagination.

Time for a scene change.

He took a last lingering toke, then pinched off the ember. Sparks tumbled to the rough-hewn floor and he stamped them under his boot. He thought of Shelley and sheepskin, then started typing, two-finger, fast.

Doug Hamilton lay naked before the fire, sipping champagne, watching Sharon as she slipped out of scant undergarments. Her skin was dark, her eyes a rich moss-green, her lips full and moist. She moved with slow, erotic grace, turning, bending, giving her man a lingering view of all her lovely parts. Now she draped herself over him, tenting his face with her luxurious black mane, brushing his lips with kisses like velvet. He set his champagne aside but the glass tipped over, sending amber fingerlets bubbling across the rustic wood floor.

The cabin belonged to Doug's brother. And Doug had it for the next six days; the cabin and Sharon and miles of idyllic isolation. Even the storm seemed perfect for their first night alone. It drew them closer, intensified the hearth-side warmth of the place.

Darrin paused, slapping his hands together with malicious delight. "Got it up yet, Dougie?" he said to the typed page. "I hope so, because pretty soon, 'It' is gonna yank it off for you." He cackled. He was ripped. His stomach growled. His mouth was parched, his eyelids leaden. He grabbed the box of Fritos off the table by the Underwood and dug in.

Munchies, Manfred.

Now he looked at the page, deciding whether or not to allow

Doug Hamilton his nookie before becoming an hors-d'oeuvre for a mutant. He considered constructing a full page of gruesomely detailed hardcore horror; even worse, he weighed the possibilities of Sharon and the thing—catchy title—*Sex Slave of the Mud Lake Mutant.*

"Whoa, boy," he said to his reflection in the window. "You're decompensating now. You got a good little monster tale going here. Don't screw it up."

He wiped his fingers on his jeans and typed, deciding he'd make the cabin in the story identical to the one he was in (except warmer), recalling what a wise old English prof had told him: *Write what you know.* And he wanted to use the door banging open in the wind. That had been suitably freaky. That would be how the eating-machine got in. Then it would creep, or maybe ooze, into the kitchen, hide around the corner while Doug went back to the fireplace . . .

A deliberate scratching sound made Darrin turn on his chair.

"Who's there?"

The words hung on the chill air. Now the scratching came again, on the apex of a powerful gust, and Darrin noticed the branches of a nearby tree scraping the north window.

"Paranoid," he mumbled. "Par-a-*noid.*"

He thought about the scaly Mud Lake Mutant. And typed.

The cabin door swung open with a nerve-jangling crash, making the lovers yelp in fear. Snow billowed into the room on sub-zero gusts.

"The damn door blew open," Doug said, annoyed and at the same time relieved to have a simple explanation for the startling intrusion. He grabbed his housecoat and pulled it on, noticing the spilled champagne and the oddly crimson hue it had created on the floorboards. That it looked like a pool of blood chilled him in a manner distinct from that caused by the bracing air. Just an illusion of color caused by the reflection of the fire, he decided, and

started along the hall to the door, his knees and ankles burning in the glacial wind.

Sharon curled closer to the fire. The fright had destroyed her mood.

Doug pushed the door shut, fired the heavy bolt and cursed under his breath. The keen pitch of arousal he'd been reaching had evaporated. He knew it would be the same for Sharon.

He noticed the odor first, like fish gone over. Then, as he minced around the patina of snow in the hallway, he noticed something else, beneath his bare feet: an icy, gelatinous film, like the goo on refrigerated turkey.

What the hell . . .?

The sound came next, a boggy slithering punctuated by stertorous breathing . . .

Darrin paused. There was an abrupt lull in the wind, and that bothered him. Because that scratching sound was there again. Only now, in this eerie quiet, it seemed to be coming from *inside* the cabin. From the kitchen.

His breathing quickened. He rose off the chair, remaining in a tense crouch. He grabbed a length of birch off the wood pile, liking its heft.

"Shelley?"

No answer. Of course. He'd bolted the door from the inside.

The wind held its curious silence, as if waiting. In the distance, the wolf howled its haunting cry. Birch, blackened and glowing, crackled in the fireplace.

Darrin tiptoed toward the kitchen, holding his breath. Floorboards creaked under his weight, the sound amplified in the expectant calm. It was as if some celestial film crew had switched off the machinery of a simulated blizzard: *Scene change, next night, dead silence, cry of lone wolf.*

Darrin edged around the corner into the kitchen, brandishing the birch log.

The kitchen was empty.

He sighed, saying, "Rodents. Varmints."

But now he caught a whiff of rot. Ridiculously, he looked at the wood floor. For turkey goo. There was none.

Of course.

But what was that rancid smell?

He opened the cooler containing his provisions . . . only fresh scents from in there. This was the reek of something long dead. He wondered why he hadn't noticed it before. Maybe there *had* been a rodent—a field mouse maybe, frozen to death in some dark corner of the cabin in December or January—that had begun to rot over the course of the week he'd been heating the place.

He opened the cupboard under the sink, rooted around, found nothing, shrugged. He continued through the kitchen, then along the hallway to the main room.

His eye caught movement now, something so fleeting it could've been a hallucination. He prayed it *had* been. He noticed it as he stepped out of the hallway, something black and glistening, snake-like, whipping around the corner into the south section of the cabin where the typewriter sat on a makeshift desk.

Darrin wished he hadn't smoked that reefer.

He waited, listening. The wind had resumed its former pitch, and Darrin welcomed that now. It obscured the smaller cabin noises that were freaking him out of his woollies. He wondered what the guy he'd bought the weed from had laced it with. He knew all kinds of illicit shit could turn up in a bag of weed, just to give it that extra kick: horse tranquilizer, low-grade smack. There must've been *something* in it, because he didn't usually hallucinate on grass.

Hallucination, right?

Crouching now, he moved to the next corner, peered along the adjoining wall. Nothing there.

Okay.

He straightened.

But what if it had slithered around the *next* corner, back into the kitchen? He checked the floorboards again: dry, unsoiled.

What if...?

Are you going whacko, Keene? Forget it. Write!

A noise. In the kitchen. Scraping.

"Shelley?" he asked the emptiness. "If that's you screwing around, I'll—" He remembered the bolted door. Unless she—or something—had gotten in when the door blew open.

"Jesus," he said in a whisper, "what would Doug Hamilton do right now?"

Go and look. What else?

He crept back to the kitchen. Bugger-all there. Now he inched through the room to the hallway. *Nothing.* He moved quickly to the next corner, almost running. *Zip.* Then, brandishing the log and whooping like a warrior, he bolted around the entire cabin, twice, using the barn-wood corners as pivots, boots thudding the floorboards.

Halfway around the third time, he stopped by the Underwood and leaned on the desk, breathless, feeling like an idiot. A dog chasing its tail. But now he understood how Doug Hamilton would be feeling, and wanted to get it into words while it was fresh. Coming clear too, was a mental picture of the Mud Lake Monster. He took a final glance behind him—just to be sure—then sat at the typewriter, scrolled the page up on the carriage, and reread the last sentence.

The sound came next, a boggy slithering punctuated by stertorous breathing...

And now Darrin heard it.

Plain as day.

Something foul, frigid, and inhumanly powerful, took hold of

Darrin Keene's head and twisted. Darrin caught a glimpse of It before the oil lamp extinguished.

Oddly, his last thought as he looked up was: *That's It!*

On the afternoon of the next day, Shelley England followed a big yellow snow plow up Kukagami Road toward the cabin. The plow operator was her second cousin, Brad Samson, and although he wasn't supposed to, Brad veered off the main road and cleared out the three-hundred yards of trail leading to the cabin. As he reversed the machine to leave, Shelley gave him a smile that made him wish for the thousandth time since grade school that Shelley E. hadn't been born his cousin.

She parked the Civic behind the snowy hump of Darrin's Jeep. She was surprised to see the cabin door ajar. But the day was sunny and mild, as so often happened up here after a storm, and she guessed he was airing the place out. It surprised her too that he hadn't come out when the plow lumbered into the yard. Maybe he was out on the racks, catching the rays.

But now she noticed there were no footprints outside the cabin, and a vague worry came over her. Haltingly, she approached the open door.

The storm had raged for thirty-six hours, snow drifting most of the way up the north wall of the cabin. The windows on that side were completely covered. Inside, the hallway was darkly shadowed.

Shelley stepped in. "Darrin?"

Her worry vanished when she realized he was probably just hiding. Darrin was a prankster. She liked that about him. Always a good time. But she hated being scared. Darrin loved to sneak up and goose his victims.

"Darrin? Talk to me. If you frighten me . . ."

She approached the kitchen with her back to the wall, the stench of rotten fish abrupt and powerful.

"Darrin? What have you been eating up here?"

She rounded the corner, irritated now with his silence. That was when she saw the press-back chair lying on the floor in front of the Underwood.

She screamed when she saw congealed blood tracking across the typewriter keys, and up onto the unfinished page.

The forensics team verified the blood type as Darrin's. The police found no footprints in the snow, but did notice the large, healed-over rent in the ice. When Shelley beseeched them to send in divers, they refused, saying it was too dangerous this time of year. They thought the hole in the ice was too large to have been made by a man anyway. When pressed for an alternate explanation, they could provide none. They told her if Darrin had in fact gone through the ice, there was nothing to do but wait until spring. Then, they said, his body would likely turn up in the thaw.

But it never did.

2

DUGGAN'S BOOTS

The tree stood on a grassy verge beyond the vegetable garden, which now lay fallow. Its gnarled trunk rose mightily, spreading its leafy tentacles into the late-summer sky. It dwarfed everything around it, standing tall against the horizon, by day a prodigious ballerina swaying in the breeze, at dusk a looming silhouette, by night a sleepless watchman with eyes full of history.

The little boy had always been enthralled by its dimensions, its quiet power, its majesty no matter the season. Today, he decided, he was going to walk right up to it, inspect it closely for the first time. It seemed to him, as he scrunched low to avoid the barbs of the wire fence bordering the garden, that the tree had always been there, in his memory. Its memory predated his understanding of it, his ability to name it or to liken it to the other things around him. It seemed somehow eternal. And for the longest time it had frightened him in some indefinable way. Sitting on the swing beneath the honeysuckle, looking out across the distance at the tree, he'd always felt safe from is unknown powers. But the thought of going over there—across the garden, between the rhubarb parasols, avoiding the blood-thirsty thorns of the raspberry patch to clamber over that last fence, the one made of old stumps with their twisted roots turned skyward—

that thought had always filled him with a diffuse sort of terror. What if he got close to the tree and it fell on him? What kept it standing there, creaking in defiance of the wind, sheltering the starlings, tolerating the rasp of the crow? Could it reach down with a leafy mitten and sweep him off his feet?

Today, these thoughts only heightened the adventure.

Oak, he thought, watching the toes of his sneakers sink into the rich black soil of the garden, casting a glance every now and then at the tree. His grandpa told him it was an oak tree. Grandpa died last winter, which made the boy sad. That was something else he didn't understand. Grandma had explained it by saying that when you got old, you died. But the tree was old, much older than his grandpa, and it was still alive. Yet Grandpa had died. In his bed. His mouth had been open (the little boy remembered going up there, into that room, after they'd taken the body away, and seeing Grandpa's false teeth sitting at the bottom of a glass of murky water on the bedside table) and he had just stopped breathing. "He's gone," Grandma had said. "Oh, my God, he's really gone." And for a long time after that, the little boy had been afraid to fall asleep, thinking he might forget, like Grandpa had done, and stop breathing in the night.

A light breeze cut the liquid heat of the August sun. It cooled the band of sweat on the boy's freckled forehead and set the high branches of the tree to a chattering murmur, as if secret messages passed from leaf to leaf.

And suddenly he was there, over the stump fence at the base of the tree, stumbling in awe over its curled toes, craning his neck to view its hazy crown. It was the biggest living thing he'd ever seen. And, he thought happily, it was safe. It didn't want to hurt him. He started to circle its woody girth. It seemed to just go round and round. What he found on the other side surprised him. There was a hole there, low and arch-shaped, at the tree's base. It seemed at once inviting and forbidding. A small boy could just fit . . .

He stepped back, considering. Clover and paintbrush and

goldenrod dappled the grass that reached past his knees. It was dark in there. Was it hollow? He knew what hollow meant—chocolate Easter bunnies were hollow.

A crow called, soared, picked a high branch and lit on it, looking down at him now with haughty black eyes.

He knelt, peered into darkness, icy fingers walking his spine as he crawled inside. It was cooler in here than outside, but it wasn't as dark as he'd thought. Light came in through the arch in a dusty column and made a neat line across his bare knees. There was an odor in here he'd never experienced, something damp and old. And it wasn't scary at all. It felt . . . safe. Cozy and comfortable. Private. From now on, this would be his secret place. He nestled his back into the shadowy wall.

Soon he began to nod, curling his fingers into the soft earthen floor, wondering what the great oak might have seen since that forgotten day its first leaves broke ground . . .

A sound, closing from a distance, low thunder setting the boy's world atremble. He poked his head outside. Strange—the air was *cold* now, and fine snow dusted everything around him. The garden and the root fence were gone.

Horses, he thought, logy with sleep. The sound was the gallop of horses, many hooves drumming the earth. Now they appeared, cresting a nearby rise, stomping across the frozen ground. The boy bumped his head pulling it back inside.

The horses were ridden by men in black hats. He couldn't count yet, but thought there were at least ten. They were dressed . . . different, funny, like cowboys on TV. Guns hung in leather holsters on their hips. Their faces were set, angry. Except one man: he looked pale and scared. He wore no hat and his holster was empty. His hands were tied with coarse rope.

Now the men circled the tree and dismounted, all but the frightened man. He stayed in the saddle on a jittery charcoal horse. The little boy was frightened now too, afraid these grim, silent men would catch him, find his secret hideaway in the tree.

A short man took the reins of the frightened man's horse, leading the animal closer to the tree. Vapor jetted from the horse's flaring nostrils. Its shuffling hooves left black patches in the snow. Another man took a rope from where it hung in a loop on his saddle, uncoiled it and tossed one end over a thick branch, then secured that end to a nearby stump.

The other end had been crafted into a noose.

Now the short man guided the charcoal horse closer, and a man dressed in black spoke, his voice dark and commanding.

"Put your head in, Tom Duggan."

The man on the horse obeyed, staring blankly ahead, not uttering a sound.

A third man snugged the noose around Duggan's neck, just beneath his bobbing Adam's apple.

"For your crime, Tom Duggan," the man in black said, "a trespass too far outside the laws that govern men to warrant the consideration of due process, your life will end here today, in full view of the Muldoon farm, in full view of Frank Muldoon here" —the man in black extended a hand toward a thin, tormented man who, to the little boy, looked eerily familiar—"whose daughter, the helpless and delicate Mary Catherine, still a child, you did rape and defile in a manner most inhumane . . ."

The little boy's breath stopped short.

" . . . for this, you shall hang by the neck in the shadow of this mighty oak until dead."

The man in black nodded, and now the short man released the reins and slapped a gloved hand against a charcoal haunch. The horse bolted, vaulting over the verge and away across the field, leaving its rider suspended in the frosty air.

Tom Duggan began a terrible, slow-motion jig. His eyes bugged as if to pop from their sockets, and his face shaded from winter pale to blood red to hideous dusk. Spittle roped from his twisted mouth. As he kicked at the air, his boots slipped from his feet, first one then the other, landing with dull thuds on the snowy ground. Tattered wool socks let gnarly toes peek through.

The men watched in grim silence. Slowly, the anger left their faces, replaced by something the boy would not understand until he was much older and life had had its way with him.

After a while, Tom Duggan became still. His eyes remained open, his tongue protruding now in a kind of hideous mocking, a purple wad grown somehow too large for his mouth.

"Cut him down," said the man in black.

The short man drew a shiny pistol. His aim was deadly accurate. The bullet tore through the rope and Tom Duggan fell to the ground in a boneless heap, landing on his scuffed leather boots.

The sharp report woke the little boy. Inside the trunk he was sweating heavily. He peered out through the arch. Tom Duggan was gone. The men and the horses were gone. And though the sky had darkened and thunder grumbled in the distance, there was no snow. It was summer again, deep August, lazy and humid and hot.

He clambered out of the hollow chamber in the oak.

A dream. It had been only a dream.

And yet . . .

His gaze drifted upward, to that brawny overhanging branch. There, rotted by the elements and frayed to near-extinction by the years, were strands of Tom Duggan's rope.

The little boy ran, scratching his bare legs on thorns and nettles, tramping through the rhubarb, tripping once in the tilled earth of the garden. He ran across the dooryard to the farmhouse, clapped through the screen door and straight into the arms of his grandma, Mary Catherine Muldoon.

He never went back to the oak, nor did he ever speak of that day. Years later, when the boy was twelve, his uncle cut the tree down for firewood.

3

ROAD RAGE

Frank Murray was southbound on Highway 69, heading home from the grocery store, when a guy in an aging silver Volvo decided he owned the passing lane. Nothing new there. The city was rife with drivers like this: assholes if they were in front of you, bullies if behind. Frank had driven the Autobahn in Germany, where the passing lane was sacrosanct. You passed, you got the hell over, and you stayed there until it was time to pass again. Simple, right?

Well, for assholes not so much.

Normally, Frank let this kind of thing go. He'd wait for a chance to pass on the right, then go about his business. Nothing to get worked up about.

But for some reason on this gorgeous spring morning—the first of its kind in a long while—this monkey just rubbed him the wrong way. Because when the guy realized Frank wanted to pass, he sidled up next to the nearest vehicle in the right lane and hung there, making it impossible to go around.

So Frank started riding the bastard's tail.

Juvenile, yes. Dangerous? As hell.

But come on, man. Get *over*. What's your problem?

Frank didn't see red, but it was akin to that. A kind of

clouding of his peripheral vision, triggered by a bitter and familiar upwelling in his gut. The animosity he felt now, though disproportionate, had been building for a long time—his entire life, if he was being honest. A pervasive feeling of frustration, a sense that no matter what he tried to accomplish, there'd always be someone or something in his way. Over the course of his adult life, he'd gone from the heady belief engendered by his parents that anything was possible, to spinning his wheels in a hell of repetition from which death seemed the only escape.

So now, at the age of forty-eight and for no rational reason, he was locked in a battle of wills with a dummy he couldn't even see, clipping along at seventy miles an hour with some very primitive areas of his brain spewing sparks. Right now, getting around this prick was all he cared about. He was on this guy's *ass*.

They crested a hill now and the traffic light at the bottom was red, a potential opportunity to sort this shit out once and for all. Frank's turnoff was a few miles past the intersection, time enough to get around this annoying little squatter and show him who's boss.

As if he'd written the script, the light turned green, the vehicle in the right lane slowed to exit the highway, and the seas parted. Frank gave the dink in the Volvo time to do the right thing . . . but no, he hung there, accelerating now, his four-cylinder shitbox spewing diesel exhaust.

Frank gunned it and went around, blowing past in his six-cylinder Sienna at eighty miles an hour. To demonstrate how it was done, he stayed in the right lane, his turnoff a half-mile ahead now.

But what the . . .?

Now the guy was riding *his* tail. And in the right lane no less.

Frank thought, *Fuck it*, and roared past his exit, heading out of the city but beyond caring. He mashed the accelerator to the mat, burying the needle in the red, and the fucker was *still* trying to catch him.

There was a side street a couple of miles ahead that branched off the highway for the length of a city block, then angled back on—and Frank decided he'd had enough. In this moment, there were two assholes screwing around at high speeds and he was one of them. If he persisted, it could only escalate; he'd seen it before. Besides, he had eggs and frozen fruit in the back seat.

He decelerated and signaled right, his point made, even if the dipshit in the Volvo didn't get it. The guy caught up and leaned on the horn as Frank made the turn, not letting up, as if Frank were the one who'd started it. He angled his body to flip the dink the bird, but it was too late, he was out of sight.

By the time Frank got to the stop sign at the top of the street, he'd made another decision.

A bad one.

Instead of turning left toward home, he hung a right, leaving a strip of rubber twenty feet long.

It was on, baby. It was *on*.

He caught up a few miles later—the guy tooling along in the right lane now like a model citizen—and got back on his tail. *Right* on his tail. It took the guy a few seconds to catch on, but then, predictably, he touched the brakes, expecting Frank to shit his pants and back off. But he was ready for a rookie move like that and decelerated in unison. They were coming up on a charter bus now and the guy pulled the same boneheaded maneuver, swerving into the passing lane, gliding up next to the bus and hanging there, blocking both lanes.

But the bus signaled right and pulled off, the road ahead open now, and the Volvo took off at speed, still hogging the left lane. Frank got on his ass again and leaned on the horn. When that didn't do it, he started flashing his high beams. This jerk was going to get over or Frank was going to know the reason why. He decided it must be an example of small-man syndrome, because he couldn't even see the guy's thick skull over the headrest.

But do you think he'd get over? Not a chance.

Frank was *way* past feeling like an asshole now. He was a goddamn *avenger*. And this taint in his rust-pocked junker was his sworn enemy. *He* was the reason Frank despised his life, the reason he felt trapped in a job he hated and a relationship that had died years ago and didn't have the sense to lie down, and if the son of a bitch didn't get the *fuck* over, Frank was gonna run him into a rock cut, pull a U-ie, and piss on his burning remains.

Now Frank noticed two things simultaneously: The guy in the car was holding a phone to his ear—Frank could see it in the guy's sideview—and there was a cop coming up hard behind them, turret lights flashing.

Oh, shit.

Frank signaled and decelerated, pulling over, thinking how lucky that Christer ahead of him was, expecting to see the guy vanish victorious into the distance. But now *he* was pulling over too, rolling to a stop fifty yards farther along the soft shoulder.

Then it dawned. The guy had called the *cops*.

Explanations marched through Frank's mind, each one lamer than the last, and he knew he was caught. A senior staff physician in the Sudbury hospital system behaving like a delinquent on a beautiful Sunday morning, risking his life and the lives of others when he should've been home by now, boiling eggs for a sensible egg-white-and-fruit breakfast.

His breath came in hot rushes as he scrambled in the dash cubby for his license and ownership, his gaze ticking from his sworn enemy—sitting smug with his flashers on—to the cop in the rearview, pulling the usual delay to call in Frank's plate number and let him stew in his own red shame.

After several minutes—time enough for Frank's rational mind to reboot—the cop swaggered up to the door and Frank opened the window. Having only glimpsed the officer's midsection in the mirror, he assumed it was a guy. But it was a broad. Dark-eyed and hard-looking, tits flattened under a navy flak jacket, a good meaty pair bulging out the armholes like pizza dough. She had a hand on her sidearm.

Frank said, "'Morning, officer," and gave her a sunny smile. It had occurred to him while he was waiting that unless she'd witnessed his antics with the Volvo, it was the asshole's word against his.

She said, "License and registration please," and Frank handed over the plastic folder he kept them in. His Canadian Medical Association membership was in there, too. More than once his status as a physician had won him slack from the local constabulary; he was counting on it doing the same today.

Examining the documents, the officer said, "Do you have any idea how fast you were going, sir?"

Frank thought, *Okay. If I can slide away from this one with a speeding ticket and a few point deductions, I'll consider it a victory.* He said, "To be honest, officer, no, I do not. It's such a nice morning, I have to admit I was daydreaming a little."

She glanced at the grocery bags on the backseat. "Where are you headed?"

"Well, home originally. But like I said, it's such a gorgeous day I decided to take a spin. Shake off the cobwebs." Sounded reasonable.

She said, "You were doing ninety-three in a fifty-five, Doctor Murray. I could impound your vehicle."

He went for charming first—"It's Frank,"—thought, *Oops, ice queen*, then said, "You're right, officer. Of course, you're right. I wasn't thinking."

But contrite wasn't going to cut it either.

"Are you aware the gentleman in the Volvo called nine-one-one, claiming you were harassing him at high speeds?"

Frank glanced at the idling Volvo. "Really? No, I wasn't aware at all. Are you sure he meant me? A gray van blew past maybe a minute before you pulled me over. Came out of nowhere."

"I didn't see any gray van, sir. Apart from this one."

"Well, I sure did. Must've come out of a side road back there."

"So you're telling me you haven't been tailgating this guy for the past ten miles?"

"Of course not. I'm a trauma surgeon. I see the carnage from that sort of behavior every week. Granted, I was speeding, but that's the extent of it."

She straightened now, glanced at the Volvo, then plucked a ticket book off her utility belt. "Wait right here, sir."

"Of course."

Frank watched her move to the Volvo, thinking, *Nice can*, pleased he'd kept his cool. He rested his elbow on the sill and watched the scene unfold.

The officer was talking to the guy now, that squinty cop expression on her face. She nodded a few times, then glanced Frank's way, and he thought, *Oh, shit, my goose is cooked*. But now the guy was gesturing, clearly furious, and the copper stiffened, touching her sidearm again, and Frank smiled, thinking, *That's it, dipshit, piss the lady off and get your dumb ass arrested*.

Now she shook her head and started back toward the van—then stopped short to respond to her two-way. Seconds later she was jogging, pausing by Frank's window to return his license and registration, saying, "It's your lucky day, Doctor, I'm on a call now. Just go home, okay?"

Then she was moving again, the junk on her duty belt jangling. She hopped into the cruiser, hit the roof lights and siren and pulled a screeching U-ie, heading back toward the city.

Frank breathed, humiliated but relieved, the unspent adrenalin having its way with him as he tucked his documents away with trembling fingers. His armpits were dripping sweat. *Jesus.* What a stupid move.

He sat a moment, staring at his feet, rehearsing what he'd say to his wife about what had taken him so long to pick up a few groceries. He was surprised when he looked up and the Volvo was still there.

What are you waiting for, you sissy prick?

As if in answer, the guy thrust a hairy forearm out the window and jabbed his middle finger in the air. Then he peeled out, spewing a rooster tail of dirt and gravel onto the van. A stone *ticked* off the windshield in front of Frank's face, making him flinch. As the Volvo vanished over a rise, Frank noticed a star-shaped chip in the glass, reflecting sunlight like a tiny diamond.

Mother-fucker.

An upwelling of rage galvanized him now, blotting out the sobering effect of recent events, and he tramped on the accelerator, raising his own clatter of gravel and abandoning any remaining vestige of common sense.

He crested the rise and spotted the Volvo a half-mile ahead. The guy was cruising along at sixty in the right lane and Frank decided it was time to get a look at him. At the moment, there were no other vehicles in the southbound lanes and Frank eased up beside him, the man tapping his fingers on the steering wheel in there, probably celebrating his petty victory. He looked about sixty-five, pasty-skinned and balding, pale blue eyes popping bright and round when they met Frank's. He mouthed what appeared to be a string of profanities and punched the go-pedal, those hairy forearms rigid now, black diesel exhaust belching from the Volvo's tailpipe.

Frank thought, *Still wanna play?* and tucked in behind him, matching his speed.

In answer, the Volvo braked so abruptly it fishtailed and Frank had to crank the wheel hard-left to avoid a collision. His heart was triphammering, a prickly sweat breaking out in his scalp, but his determination to dominate this fucker was white hot now and intensifying by the heartbeat. He'd come within an ace of rear-ending the guy at seventy miles an hour, but it gave him an insight into what he was up against. The Volvo was a beater, thirty years old if it was a day, rust-eaten and riding low to the ground. If Frank hit him from behind, in the eyes of the law it'd be his fault, and at these speeds it could put him in the hospital or worse.

Common sense tried once more to intervene, but he brushed it off like an annoying insect. He had no idea what the end game was supposed to be, all he knew was he had to see it through. He couldn't remember feeling so *alive*, seeing the world so clearly. In the beating sun, everything seemed freshly minted. The trees, the unblemished sky, even the worn blacktop gleamed as he returned to the right lane, the Volvo closing the distance now.

They played leap frog for a few miles, pushing the vehicles to perilous speeds, the lanes ahead still vacant on this pleasant Sunday morning. Despite the Volvo's apparent age, the damn thing could *go*, the driver fearless and more skilled than Frank had imagined from the look of him. The fourth time the guy came up on his left, Frank tramped the pedal to the floor and kept it there, stressing the engine to a high whine, and they ran neck-and-neck for a mile or so, until the Volvo backfired and fell back, releasing a cannon-blast of black smoke.

Frank gave a triumphant hoot and let up on the gas, holding his position in the right lane and thinking enough was enough. It was a clear victory, and with any luck the bastard had blown his engine. Frank rounded a bend and glanced in the rearview—no sign of the nutcase—thinking he'd get turned around up ahead, double back and slow down to laugh his ass off at his vanquished opponent. There was an overpass in the near distance, a string of vehicles merging southbound from the feeder lane now. He could exit onto the bridge and—

No way . . .

The Volvo popped into the rearview from around the bend, a mere speck at first but gaining fast, trailing a plume of exhaust the size of a drag chute.

Crazy son of a bitch.

There was a moment now, a dart of fear flickering through Frank's gut on a wave of nausea, and he realized he might be dealing with a psychopath here, someone prepared to take this madness lightyears beyond what he had been up for when he made the mistake of engaging. You could never tell from looking at a person. He'd seen a documentary recently on serial killers, men typically viewed by their neighbors and coworkers as quiet and unassuming, until their true natures came horrifically to light.

He began to tremble, watching the Volvo's aggressive approach and imagining the worst—the psycho finding out where he lived, breaking in and killing him and his wife in their sleep, or running him off the road *today* to roast in a fiery wreck—and he committed to one last burst of speed, aiming for the exit a half-mile distant. He'd noticed a Toronto Volvo dealership sticker on the rear bumper of the maniac's car. In all likelihood, once Frank got out of his way, the guy would continue south, feeling like he'd won. Frank no longer gave a shit. Let him think he'd come out on top.

The Volvo was almost kissing his bumper now and he decelerated to take the exit lane, watching in the sideview for the guy to blow by on the left—

But the whacko veered hard *right* onto the shoulder and came up next to him on the passenger side, hogging the exit lane, riding so close to the van Frank couldn't believe they weren't bumping elbows—and in seconds, getting off the highway was no longer an option.

Jesus Christ. This was getting *way* out of hand.

Forced to continue south, it occurred to him to call nine-one-one himself, but his cell was on the bedside table at home, jacked into the charger. And the lunatic was glued to his ass again, white-knuckling the wheel, bald head gleaming in the sunlight . . . and Frank could swear those beady eyes were flashing red.

The few alternatives he could muster marched through his mind, none of them very appealing. He could pull over, and if the guy did the same they could shout it out or maybe even duke it out, settle this once and for all. Frank had never been in an actual fist fight, but he'd studied martial arts for a few months in university. At a glance, the guy didn't look like much, but you never could tell. Maybe he'd hop out of the car with a tire iron or a knife —or worse, a handgun. The Internet was teeming with episodes of road rage gone terribly awry.

So no, stopping was out.

He could continue south at the speed limit and hope the guy got sick of the game and took off past him, jabbing all the middle fingers out the window he wanted, who gave a shit?

Or maybe, hope to see a cop and flag him down . . . but no, that could get complicated, ending with both of them arguing it out in a police station.

Shit.

He decided to slow things down, hope the guy got tired of—

Frank's body jerked in the seat. At first he thought it'd been a pothole he'd failed to notice, but no, the guy had *bumped* him. Not hard, just enough to make contact—and now he was *pushing* the damn van.

You crazy son of a whore.

Traffic was picking up now and Frank knew he was out of options. All he could do was try to lose the guy, outrun him. The Volvo was still billowing black smoke. If he ran the guy hard enough, maybe his engine really *would* pack it in, and Frank could head home and tell his wife the whole mad tale, better than trying to come up with some bullshit excuse anyway.

He started weaving in and out of traffic, the Volvo pacing him, staying on his tail.

Christ, this guy can drive.

Frank was coming up on a flatbed now, dead ahead in the right lane. He glanced in his sideview—a transport approaching at speed to pass in the left lane—and saw his next move in glorious Technicolor. At the last possible instant, he floored it, closing in tight on the flatbed before veering into the left lane in front of the transport, earning a protracted bellow on the airhorn but seeing nothing ahead but open road.

His heart was riding in his throat, his palms slippery on the wheel, but a glance in the rearview showed no sign of that bastard and his Volvo.

There was an exit ahead and Frank took it, speeding up the on-ramp, then across the overpass and around the loop into the northbound lanes. No sign of the Volvo in pursuit.

Traffic was sparse in this direction, just an old dude in an ancient Ford pickup and a school bus occupied only by the driver. Frank glanced across the median a few times, alert for his nemesis, but there was no sign of him. Probably slipped under the overpass while Frank was crossing it. And good riddance.

He began to relax, his heart rate settling, the shakes easing off. There was no swell of victory, only relief and embarrassment. Like a punk teenager with a chip on his shoulder, he'd willfully engaged in impetuous behavior with a whole host of potential consequences—

A plume of smoke ahead in the southbound lanes, the transport he'd cut off motionless now, hazards blinking, the driver on the blacktop popping road flares. Frank slowed, wondering if he'd caused an accident, that sick feeling brewing in his guts again.

Once past the transport, he saw what had happened and his gorge rose in his throat.

The Volvo was wedged under the rear end of the flatbed as far back as the door handles, the roof resting on the metal bed as if the vehicle had been surgically bisected. The driver's head, visible through the blood-spattered side window, rested on the lip of the ramp two feet from the rest of his body, the face angled toward Frank, those pale eyes vacant and wide. Flames licked up from the engine compartment, curling around the edges of the truck bed.

Traffic was suspended over there, oglers abandoning their vehicles to gather in knots for a closer look. A few glanced Frank's way, breaking the grim spell, and he accelerated away from the chaos, numb with terror and disbelief.

When the scene had dwindled behind him, he pulled over and vomited onto the blacktop.

He drove home in a fog of anxiety and dread, head throbbing, the acid aftertaste of puke in his mouth. How many people had witnessed his crazed behavior? Were there traffic cameras on highways now? Oh, God, *dash* cams. Everybody and his brother had a dash cam. And that lady cop. Had she recorded his information? At the very least she'd run his plate number.

I'm fucked. I am so fucked*!*

His wife was on him the instant he came through the door.

"What took you so long? Why are you sweating? Oh, Jesus, you smell like vomit. Have you been drinking? On a Sunday *morn*ing?"

He did his best to placate her, saying he'd had a flat tire in the grocery store parking lot and had to change it himself because his phone was on the charger and he couldn't call triple-A. He said it took forever in that hot sun, the lugs tight as hell, his back killing him, and he believed he got a touch of sunstroke because he threw up on the drive home. She said, "Not in the van, I hope," and he said no, out the window, and if she didn't mind he was going to go upstairs and lie down, pop a Gravol and maybe take a nap. Huffing, she snatched the grocery bags and marched off to the kitchen, saying, "I guess I'll put this stuff away, then. Did you get garlic like I asked?"

He hadn't, but he said nothing. Let her figure it out.

He went to his office, a cozy niche facing the backyard, and locked the door. Years ago the space had been intended as a nursery, but Frank had turned up sterile, his sperm count negligible, and he believed Valerie had never forgiven him for that. He'd suggested adoption, but she'd been vehemently opposed, saying it had to be her own child or forget about it. Artificial insemination from an anonymous donor evoked a similar response. In Frank's mind, that day eighteen years ago when the test results came in had torpedoed their relationship, Val morphing overnight from the selfless, loving, sexy girl he'd married into a moody, scornful narcissist who blamed him for everything and reveled in jabbing him with less-than-subtle criticisms at the slightest provocation.

He sat at the desk and opened his laptop, thinking, *That's the least of your worries now, buddy*. Every time he blinked, he saw that decapitated head and its pale, accusing eyes.

He searched 'traffic cameras' first, learning there were all kinds —red-light, speed, ANPRs (Automatic Number Plate Recognition), traffic flow, video and still—and they were ubiquitous, many monitored by AI.

God damn it.

No matter how he juggled the details in his mind, it all boiled down to the same conclusion: Sooner or later the cops were going to appear at his front door, charge him with vehicular manslaughter or worse, drag him through the court system for months, then throw him in federal prison for the rest of his days.

As he stared at the screen, Frank Murray experienced a kind of seismic shift, a sense that every experience and ambition he'd had to this point in his life had been drawn under and obliterated by the weight of what he now must face. He couldn't conceive of a way around it. It was simply a matter of time.

He did another search, this one cementing his fears:

In Ontario, a fatal dangerous driving incident typically results in the charge of Dangerous Operation of a Conveyance Causing Death under section 320.13(3) of the Criminal Code of Canada. This is a severe indictable offence carrying a maximum penalty of life imprisonment, with other potential charges including criminal negligence causing death.

Life imprisonment. *Jesus.* He was forty-eight years old, just turned. The men in his family typically lived well into their eighties and nineties. His dad passed at ninety-six, his grandfather at ninety, the majority of his uncles in their late eighties. Which meant he could be locked up for as many as *forty years.*

Uh-huh. No way.

There was a sudden expulsive pressure low in Frank's gut and he unlocked the door and sprinted to the bathroom across the hall, getting his pants down just in time to blast the bowl full of mud. Filmed in sweat, he lingered on the john, head-in-hands, until he was certain he was through, then got the paperwork done and hobbled back to the office, lightheaded and moaning. He relocked the door and sat in the chair, thinking, *Forty fucking years . . .*

It had occurred to him on the drive home to head straight to O.P.P. headquarters and turn himself in, thinking it might be his best bet. Thinking maybe they'd cut him some slack. After all, it *was* an accident. Put him under house arrest maybe, suspend his driver's license for life, levy a huge fine. He'd been smart with his money. Between the house, his other properties and his retirement savings, he could probably muster a couple million, maybe even two-and-a-half if Val pitched in. He could explain to the judge that the guy in the Volvo had provoked the entire incident, given him no choice but to . . .

No. Scratch that. He'd seen enough TV shows to realize any competent prosecutor would hang him out to dry if he tried to float such a lame justification.

"Why didn't you just pull over, Doctor Murray? How dare you insult this court and the victim's grieving family with such a juvenile defense? *He* started it? Come on. You're an educated man, you should know better."

Bottom line, his heedless actions had cost a man his life. *Period.*

He leaned back in the chair now, the joints in his spine popping in protest, his mind insisting on sprinting ahead, conjuring the worst . . .

The humiliation of being led down the porch steps handcuffed and shackled, the neighbors looking on, whispering, Val leaning dry-eyed in the doorway with her arms crossed. Escorted by mute officers to the lockup downtown, marched through the sally port to a cell stinking of piss and stale sweat. Would he get his own cell or would there be other criminals there, *real* criminals, eyeballing him with rape and torture in their hearts? He wasn't kidding himself. He was out of shape, sporting a paunch, taking two meds a day for hypertension, another for cholesterol, and had no idea how to defend himself, those few karate lessons so far in the past he could barely recall a single move. Then the public spectacle of the trial. A jury of his peers. The withering stares of the man's family. The outcome a foregone conclusion. The judge reading the verdict, and the final *crack!* of the gavel—

A knock at the door now, three staccato strikes startling him out of his skin, a futile twist of the knob and then Val's voice, sharp and annoyed.

"What are you *do*ing in there? Why is this door locked? I thought you were taking a nap."

Frank snapped the laptop shut and let her in.

Over the interminable days that followed, Frank Murray withdrew into a pit of dread and sleepless paranoia. On his first day back to work—the Monday following the incident—he was walking past the surgical waiting area and saw a cop in uniform talking to the desk clerk. He stopped mid-stride and averted his gaze, doing an abrupt about-face to head back to the locker room. He lingered there a while, pacing in the bathroom, then called the desk clerk, doing his best to sound casual asking what the cop was all about. It turned out the officer was accompanying a convict slated for exploration and repair of a stab wound, the clerk saying, "You should see this guy, Doctor Murray. Tattoos and piercings all over the place. He's not your patient, is he?" Frank told her no, he was calling because he'd just vomited and believed he was coming down with a stomach flu. He asked her to cancel his list for the day, changed back into his civvies and drove home. Thankfully Val was out, a Post-it note on the foyer mirror saying she was at her sister's place and would probably spend the night. He called the department head and his own office to let everyone know he'd be out of circulation until further notice. That had been a week ago.

In the interim, he'd spent the majority of his time facing his laptop screen. There were numerous initial reports of the grisly accident, complete with chilling cell-phone photos and post-event video footage provided by rubberneckers at the scene, but no mention of a high-speed chase or the involvement of a third vehicle. One report identified the victim as fifty-six-year-old Christian Mäkinen, a Toronto public school janitor and father of three. Another account stated the possibility the driver was under the influence, but couldn't confirm until the forensic report became available. The same article revealed a registered handgun had been found properly stored in the trunk of the vehicle, the driver apparently a target-shooting enthusiast. All perfectly legal.

Frank thought, *I figured that guy was armed.*

Despite the open-and-shut flavor of the media coverage—the unofficial consensus being a freak accident related to aggressive driving and a possible DUI—Frank was unbuoyed by the lack of mention of another vehicle, certain the lady cop would figure it out sooner or later, or some concerned citizen with a dashcam would recall seeing two maniacs playing Formula 1 miles before the accident site and submit the footage to police. To Frank, it all seemed as inevitable as death itself.

He spent the endless nights on the fold-out couch in the office, the support rods punishing his back, his mind spinning out frightful images informed by untold hours spent scouring the Internet, all of it leading to the same inescapable conclusion: a life sentence in a maximum-security federal prison, the most likely destination in his case being Millhaven Institution in Bath, Ontario.

Millhaven.

Even the name sounded terrifying. Photos showed a grim sprawl of grey buildings low to the ground, reminiscent of Nazi work camps, with tall black fences topped with razor wire and flanked by fortified gun turrets.

He binge-watched *Inside The World's Toughest Prisons*, all seven seasons, and viewed dozens of first-person accounts on YouTube of the horrors and defilements of federal incarceration:

rape and stabbings, torture and beatings, no place to hide, no one to protect you.

Forty years . . . I can't do it . . .

It occurred to him one late night that his best option might be to flee the continent. Find a non-extradition country and hole up there for the duration. The notion had such a great and obvious appeal, he rolled off the couch and dug out his passport. *Expired. Shit.* A new one would take weeks to acquire. Maybe he could live off-grid somewhere instead, like the far north, one of those remote villages, learn to live off the land . . .

The complexities and foolhardiness of these thoughts finally husked him out, and he lay curled on the couch and wept until exhaustion claimed him for a few merciful hours.

By the end of the second week, Frank had lost fifteen pounds, hadn't slept over an hour straight in days, and had run out of excuses to give to his wife. On the Friday night, when he passed out on the bathroom floor from exhaustion and dehydration, she warned that if he didn't smarten up soon and get back to work, she was going to call Algoma Psychiatric and arrange for a 72-hour hold for clinical assessment.

When his best friend from med school, Pat Kelly, arrived unannounced from Kingston the following afternoon, he told Frank that Val had called the night before and explained the situation as she saw it. Frank apologized for the unwarranted intervention, saying he was fine, it was just a stomach flu. But Pat, a gastroenterologist, wasn't buying it.

After downing a few beers with his old buddy on the deck, Frank decided to fess up. He trusted Pat implicitly, and as he spoke, realized that talking it out was probably the best thing he could do right now. Surprising him, Pat's take on the situation gave him genuine hope.

"I think you're worrying yourself sick over nothing."

"Seriously?" Frank said. "I went full *Mad Max* with this guy for at least thirty miles. All kinds of other people must've seen us."

"So? How often do you see that kind of shit on the highways?"

"All the time."

"And do you think twice about it?"

"I guess not."

"No. Be*cause* you see it all the time. You shake your head, think *Assholes*, and go about your business. Right?"

Frank took a swig of *Stella*, then said, "You're right."

"Of course I'm right. You need to let this go, man. How long's it been?"

Feeling the alcohol now, Frank said, "Two weeks tomorrow."

"So don't you think that by now, if they had anything on you at all, you'd at least've been interviewed?"

"I suppose. But what about that lady cop? I tried to bullshit her, but I could tell she saw right through me."

"So what? Listen, my brother-in-law's a cop. He tells me all the time about the nonsense he has to put up with on a daily basis, and how if he didn't let most of it slide he'd be buried in paperwork for the rest of his days. You said she got pulled away on a call, right?" Frank nodded. "Well, in all likelihood it was an actual emergency. She was probably relieved. Instead of baking in the sun listening to you two idiots lie through your teeth, she got to go ahead and do something useful with her day."

"But she called in my plate number—"

"Frank, that's routine. She's just checking your license and registration status, looking for warrants or suspensions, unpaid fines, that kind of shit. If your nose is clean on all of that . . .?"

"It is."

"Then forget about it, man. You didn't cause that bastard to rear end the flatbed. You simply got out of his way so he couldn't do the same to you. Just sit tight and don't panic. You'll see. Everything's gonna work out fine."

"You really think so?"

"*Yes.* Now listen. I'm going to tell your wife I'm almost a hundred percent certain you have a gastric ulcer. I'm going to write you a prescription; you're going to fill it and keep the pills in your locker at work. Flush 'em down the toilet in a month. I'll tell her if your 'symptoms' persist after that, I'll bring you down to KGH for a scope. Okay?"

"Okay, Pat. Thanks. Thanks a lot."

"My pleasure, buddy. Now who do I have to blow to get another beer?"

Frank scooped a beer out of the cooler by his feet and handed it to his friend.

They were quiet for a while after that, enjoying the evening breeze, crickets and peepers in the nearby fields warming up for the long night ahead.

Now Pat said, "Took his head clean off, huh?"

Frank nodded. "Grisly shit, man. Never seen anything like it. I have no idea why he didn't hit the brakes."

"The van was probably blocking his view. Those flatbeds are low riders. Dummy probably hit the gas when he realized you were changing lanes."

"Jesus."

~

In the face of his old friend's assurances, Frank began to think he might actually be off the hook. He just had to sit tight, like Pat said, keep his head down and wait it out.

Gradually, over the course of the next several days, he began to feel more like himself, his appetite returning, the fear of grievous consequences supplanted by sporadic spasms of guilt. But now he fought back. Was *any* of this even his fault? Well, partially, yes, but Mr. Mäkinen had been a willing participant in a hazardous game *he* had instigated. And who had been most responsible for the mad escalations? The man should've backed off when his chariot backfired and fell behind. But no, the crazy prick couldn't let it go. *He* had pushed it from a typical traffic fracas to a full-scale blood battle. And was it a crime if an enemy was slain during wartime? Frank didn't think so.

By Tuesday of the third week, all mention of the incident had vanished from the media, replaced by florid accounts of wider tragedies and perpetual political mayhem. That afternoon, Frank called his office and told his secretary he'd be in the next morning to see any scheduled patients.

For a while, life returned to something like normal.

Early the next month, the doorbell rang on a drizzly Saturday morning, a single resonant chime. Frank heard his wife holler, "Are you going to get that?" and ignored her. He was upstairs in the office catching up on his charts and she was *down*stairs doing squat. After the second ring, he heard her huff and march out to the foyer, saying, "Now what the hell could *they* want?"

Curious, he went to the master bedroom at the front of the house and peered out the window.

There was a Sudbury Police cruiser idling at the curb.

Frank's throat stoppered and he lunged away from the window, adrenalin surging, his worst fears explosively unearthed.

Oh Jesus they found me.

Valerie Murray opened the front door and greeted the two officers, one male, the other female. Self-conscious about the mess of the house, she stepped out onto the porch, pulled the door partway shut and inquired as to why they were here.

They introduced themselves, then the male officer said, "We're canvassing the neighborhood for possible information about a missing child." He held up a photo of a redheaded girl of about six.

Valerie said, "Oh, my God, that's Mary Bedward's daughter. They live just down the street."

The female officer said, "That's correct. Have you by any chance seen—?"

A gunshot rang out from inside the house and both officers drew their weapons. The male officer told Valerie to stay put while they checked it out but she ran ahead, calling Frank's name, up the stairs to the office door—locked from the inside—then made way for the male officer, the man booting the door *hard* now, the female officer poised with her weapon ready as the hinges let go and the door angled inward all askew and Frank was on the floor in there with his face missing, half his head and a deep scoop of his neck spattered across the room in a grisly supernova, strings of it drizzling from the ceiling. The shotgun his grandfather had bequeathed to him lay across one splayed arm, a curl of smoke issuing from each barrel.

Valerie said, "I told him to get rid of that damn gun," and fainted dead away.

While the male officer tended to her, his partner peeled a Post-it note off a glass-fronted bookcase. Scrawled on it in red ink were the words, *I'm sorry. I didn't mean for it to happen.*

Mary Bedward's daughter Chelsea turned up on her own later that day. She'd fallen asleep in the next-door neighbor's treehouse.

4

THE APOLOGY

I guess being alone in this shoebox apartment was the worst. That and the awful restlessness of my late-night visitor. She was a big part of the reason I decided to battle the odds and apply for Jessica's adoption. It was a wild idea from the start. Thinking back, I can scarcely believe I dreamed it up. And even though it didn't work out exactly like I planned, I thank God I did what I did. I really thank God.

Jesse's here with me now, asleep in the spare bedroom. Tonight's her first night away from the hospital. Four long, loveless years in that place. It turns my heart cold to think of it. I can hear her raspy little snores from where I'm sitting. I guess I'll have to buy a humidifier for the poor thing. It's so dry in that back room.

The first time I saw Jesse was the day they brought her up to the children's ward. She was only six months old then. She looked so perfect, I fell in love with her right away: olive skin, tiny pink hands and feet, hair so blonde it was silver. And those blue, blue eyes. I still believe I'm the only one she's ever really looked at with those angel eyes. Most of the time they stay rolled up in their sockets, showing their underbellies.

It's a common thing at the chronic center, kids like Jesse, born without all of their faculties, left by parents to die or just vegetate in one of those awful cage beds. That's what they kept Jesse in. It's like a crib, only the bars go right up over the top. Like a monkey cage, only not so roomy. She threw a lot of fits the first couple years; that was why they put her in the cage. She doesn't throw so many now, thank goodness, not since they got her meds squared away. They're godawful to witness, those fits. Her tiny body comes right off that rubber mattress, I swear, just like that kid in *The Exorcist*. She hisses and growls like that too, and her eyes flip way back in her head. One night she bit her tongue so hard they had to put stitches in it. I was there that time, so the doctor let me hold her head while he sewed her up.

That's what scares me most about having her here, those damned fits. The nurses told me what to do, but it still scares me. Now that I have her, I believe I'd just die if I ever lost her.

Her natural mother was only a kid, sixteen or seventeen at the most, so full of dope she couldn't even write her name on the release forms. It's a terrible thing to say, but little Jesse was probably better off on the ward than with that creature. But that's all behind her now, thank heaven, now that she's mine.

I work up at the chronic hospital, have since I was eighteen, almost twenty-seven years. It doesn't seem that long somehow. I quit for a while when things were good between Hal and me, and he was working steady. I was lucky they took me back when the bum started drinking again. Hal never did anything by half measures. Once he found his stride, it only took him a couple years to drink himself to death. And good riddance.

I'm a cleaning lady up there, night shifts mostly. I'm in charge of the children's floor. The money isn't great, but it keeps the roof up and the belly warm. It's a job. What can a body expect with no high school or college degree? There'll be a little extra now that I've got my sweet Jesse. The Children's Aid promised a check regular, every month. And my sister says she'll help out all she can. She'll be staying over, nights that I work. Dear Angie.

Like I said at the beginning, it was the visitor got me started on the idea. Mind, the first time I saw her I nearly jumped out of my skin. I never was one to believe in ghosts, that's for certain. But when you see one up close, face to face, well, the eye don't lie, like my papa always said. Seeing is believing. Though I guess 'face to face' is the wrong phrase to use with this sorry little shade. You see, my ghost has no head.

It's small, a child I expect, a little girl, and it lives . . . can you say 'lives' when you're talking about an apparition? Anyway it 'stays' in the back of my bedroom closet. I was set to pick up and move the first couple of times she appeared, but then I got curious. She meant me no harm, that much I could tell. And there was this terrible loneliness about her. I guess I felt sorry for her.

She only appears at night. I can tell when she's going to come because the room gets cold. Even in summer, when you suffer with the heat in these airless apartments, my skin goes all goosey just before she comes. One night—it was the middle of March, mind you, and cool down here anyway—I could actually see my breath when she popped out of the closet.

I had my sister over for a week after that one, so she could see it too. But it won't come out when I've got company, I know that now. Angie searched the apartment for liquor one day when I was out doing groceries; I could tell. She thinks I'm crazy. Maybe she's right.

It was when my visitor spoke the first time that I got the idea. I won't forget that night if I live to be a hundred. I swear, my windpipe nearly sealed over when I heard that terrible little voice. Why, there, my skin's gone all goosey just thinking about it.

"I'm sorry, Mommy," she said, and Oh, God, there was pure terror in that voice. *"I'm sorry."*

You might wonder how a thing with no head can speak. All I can tell you is I could hear the voice, but the sound was sort of on the inside, like a loud thought. That's the only way I can think to describe it.

After that, I decided to try and adopt Jessica. Like I said before, it was a crazy idea. But it was worth a shot, wasn't it? And even though I failed at one important part, isn't it better to have her here with me and out of that Godless place? I believe it is.

Despite the problems they said I'd have trying to adopt Jesse—I'm a widow, pushing fifty and living just this side of the poverty line, to list just a few—I think they gave her to me because they know I love her. Doctor Reed especially. I'm sure his good word helped. I've almost lost my job a couple of times over Jesse, sitting with her, rocking her when I should've been doing the floors. Lord, how I used to rush through my work just to spend an hour with her before coming home to sleep the sunshine away. Sometimes, I honestly got the feeling she knew I was there. That she understood, felt my love. After all, true love is magical. She would cry when I put her back in that cage. Not cry . . . she doesn't cry the way we think of it. It's a kind of animal sound, lowing. It breaks your heart, believe me.

The wild, really nutty part of my plan was this: I figured if I could trap my little ghost somehow, then maybe, just *maybe*, I could get her into Jesse. Get her to be the child's soul. When you look at Jesse, you don't need an education to see the poor thing has no soul. And she's so perfect otherwise, her body I mean, not all twisted like so many of the others up there. When I told Angie about the idea, she sort of backed away and said, "Tabby, you watch too much TV." That's probably true. I'm sure I never would've thought of it if I hadn't seen some of those shows, you know, those horror shows, that sci-fi stuff. When you're alone you watch a lot of TV.

The kicker was how to catch her.

Thinking about it got me wondering how she died. I thought of asking the landlord about previous tenants, but he's a scabby old lech who keeps telling me he's got a thing for chubby broads. Well, this is one plus-size gal he'll never get his feelers into. Not a chance.

I took a trip to the public library and waded through a bunch of microfilmed newspapers—a child murder in a town like Sudbury would make big news—but no luck there. I gave that up for a bad habit when I started seeing double. Then I did ask a few questions: the police, neighbors. But nobody knew anything. Or if they did, they were keeping it to themselves.

Still, it was hard not to wonder. Seeing as this ghost had no head, some pretty gruesome possibilities came to mind. I never had any children, but even so, it's hard to imagine harming one, let alone committing murder. The wondering started to work its way into my sleep. There, in the nightmare, the imagination runs wild.

How do you *catch* a ghost? I couldn't come up with a single idea. I did notice one thing about her, though, something I thought I could use. When she appears—and she's always wearing that same powder blue skirt and white ruffled blouse—it seems she can't just pass through things, the way you'd expect a ghost could. Once, she bumped into the bureau, and even though I could see right through her, she didn't just blend into it. She turned away from it. The only place she vanishes is inside the closet. One time I tried to get past her, to shut the closet door, but she got frightened and rushed back inside. Another time I rigged a crude sort of pulley affair, so I could close the door from my bed. But she wouldn't come out, not until I took the pulley away. It was like she knew.

Then it came to me.

And to my mind, at the time anyway, it seemed like a foolproof plan. Once I was set up, though, it took nearly a week for her to appear.

But last night, she came.

And I *caught* her.

I don't mind saying, by the time last night rolled around, I was getting pretty discouraged. I figured if I didn't nab her soon I never would, since Jesse was coming home today and that little spook refuses to come out when I'm not alone. It was my last chance. So I decided to sit up all night and watch for her. God knows, I might've slept through all kinds of her blind wanderings in the ten years I've been a tenant here and never even known.

I sat in bed against a heap of pillows, a pot of coffee on the nightstand beside me. I tried to read, but by half-past three the coffee pot was empty and my eyes were heavy with sleep. I kept nodding off. Between shifts like that, it's hard to get back on a normal person's schedule. Sometimes I can sit up late with the TV, but I didn't want to use it for fear of scaring her off with the noise.

Just before dawn, that frightful, pleading voice cut me like a razor.

"I'm sorry, Mommy . . . so sorry . . ."

I was right off to sleep before that, still propped against the headboard. When I opened my eyes, she was standing beside me, not two feet away, those tiny arms outstretched like she wanted me to pick her up and give her a hug.

When I popped up and reached for the Electrolux I'd left by the bed, her arms came smartly down by her sides, her hands balled into fists, and she started making a terrible animal sound, like what Jesse used to do when I put her back in her cage.

For the first time since the start, I was terrified of my little spook. Not of what she might do to me so much. No. It was more what she stood for that got inside me like a dead thing, the empty place she came from, the senseless violence that must have put her there.

The vacuum was already plugged in, the bag inside brand new. I grabbed the flexible hose, hit the power button and aimed the nozzle right at her. She took a clumsy step toward the closet, but the suction already had her. In a wink, she vanished through that nozzle like a discarded bit of cloth. I left the power on until I had the machine open and my hand over the mouth of the bag, then I slapped a square of duct tape over the hole.

I had her.

I dressed in a panic. Amazing what you don't think of in advance. If I'd had my wits about me, I'd've left my street clothes on. I kept the vacuum bag beside me the whole time, talking to it, reassuring it. Then I called a cab and had the driver take me up to the hospital. I bet he had a story to tell over coffee at the end of his shift, a fat lady whispering to a vacuum bag in the middle of the night.

I guess I never believed I'd catch her, not really, because there was one important part of the plan I hadn't considered: now that I had her, how was I supposed to get her to take up lodgings inside my sweet Jessica? My mother called me an idiot once; I don't think once was enough. Going up to level five on the elevator, I decided I'd just have to play it by ear.

There was grey dawn light sifting through the blinds by the time I got to Jesse. She was lying on her side with her back tight to the bars, her tiny wrists all red from tugging at those godforsaken restraints. Her eyes were rolled back, like usual, and the poor thing was drooling. Somewhere on the other side of the ward a child was crying, the most mournful sound you'd ever want to hear. And all of a sudden, I couldn't wait to get Jesse as far away from there as my meager savings would allow. Right then, I didn't even care if my little scheme worked or it didn't. I just wanted us out of there.

I'm glad none of the nurses happened by when I was doing this, because they might've reported me as crazy and I'd've lost Jesse before I even had her. I wasn't supposed to pick her up until ten.

I set the vacuum bag on a chair and lifted Jesse out of the cage. I sat with her a while, rocking her, the bag wedged between her heart and mine. And I swear that bag felt cold, like it had frozen food inside.

I talked to Jesse, talked to the bag, rocked, prayed. Then, around eight-thirty, I decided I'd just have to gamble. I stuck the hole in front of Jesse's little mouth, ripped off the tape, and gave the bag a squeeze.

Nothing came out. And Jesse didn't change.

I should've known.

I cried some, tossed the bag in the waste bin, then joined the day girls for coffee. They brought my spirits up some. At ten, I collected my baby and cabbed home.

Like I said, it was a crazy idea.

"I'm sorry, Mommy . . . so sorry . . ."

I dropped the magazine I was reading and pushed away from the table, that voice getting right inside me. I thought at the very least I'd gotten rid of my ghost.

But it was back.

And it was in my baby's room.

I rushed to the bedroom door and swung it open, fearful of what the spirit might do, afraid I'd angered it, harmed it in some way, and now it meant to avenge itself on Jessica.

I stood at the foot of the single bed in shock. It took me a moment to move again, and when I did I had to grope my way through a blur of tears.

Jesse was sitting up in the middle of the bed, all by herself. Her clear blue eyes were wide open, tear-filled and fixed on mine, and her tiny, perfect arms were outstretched, as if she wanted to be picked up and hugged.

"I'm sorry, Mommy . . ." she said, fear making her new voice tremble, ". . . so sorry."

I scooped her into my loving arms. "It's okay, my angel," I whispered. "Hush now. There's nothing to be sorry about. Nothing at all."

5

FRIGIDAIRE

According to his dad, Wayne's interest in Nazism was a transient adolescent thing, a morbid fascination—nothing to get worked up about. In his mother's opinion, it was a sick and potentially dangerous obsession.

It all began five years ago, in the late 60's, when Wayne was nine. He'd been sitting in front of the TV one Sunday evening, half-watching a black-and-white documentary on Nazi Germany. The narrator had been outlining the fate of traitors in Hitler's regime, and a truck pulling into an abandoned courtyard caught Wayne's attention. A squad of brownshirts followed, goose-stepping with mechanical precision, leading a man with bound wrists and a burlap bag over his head. They clopped to a halt behind the truck in the courtyard; it looked like a tow truck, but the winch arm had a noose dangling from the end. One of the soldiers looped the noose around the prisoner's neck and—right there on TV for all the world to see—the winch arm angled upward and the man was hung until dead.

It had been a slow, kicking, wriggling death which had both horrified and fascinated Wayne. From that day on, his interest in all things Nazi had grown and grown. Now, his attic bedroom looked like it belonged to a practicing member of the Hitler Youth.

He sat cross-legged on his antique spool bed, leafing through a dog-eared copy of a book called *The Horrors of Auschwitz*, written by a Polish pathologist who had survived its rigors. Wayne had read the old paperback numerous times; he was merely scanning it now, stopping at times to ponder bits he'd underlined in red. He was especially bewitched by a passage dealing with 'medical' experimentation, specifically, the effects of isolation and sensory deprivation. He imagined Herr Doctor Mengele sitting stone-faced at his desk, recording his observations by lamplight.

Fear is evident even before the subject is placed in the cubicle. With time, however, this fear matures into the purest breed of terror. It can be seen in the eyes, in the way the lips draw back from the teeth in a most fearsome rictus. One can readily imagine a costume ball peopled only by the subjects of this experiment. It would be a Halloween ball, and all would be wearing the same mask. It would indeed be a mad affair.

Wayne slapped the book shut. He noticed his own reflection in the bureau mirror and bared his teeth, thinking, *The Auschwitz Costume Ball*, and laughed out loud.

Now he looked around his museum-bedroom.

A leering photo of Hitler adorned the upper-right corner of the mirror. Dozens of other wartime photos were tacked helter-skelter to the slanted attic walls. An authentic Iron Cross, first class, hung in a place of honor over the study table. The top shelf of the bookcase was littered with other bits of Nazi memorabilia: brass shell casings, medals, badges, currency, a coal-scuttle helmet with a bullet hole in it. A year ago, a former Panzer gunner named Rudy Müller had loaned him a boxful of this stuff, believing it was for a school project, but a week later the man died of a heart attack in the kitchen of the burger joint he'd opened after the war, and Wayne had kept the box and all of its treasures. He was especially proud of the helmet.

But in his closet was hidden the pièce de résistance, an authentic replica of a ranking SS officer's uniform. Ironically, his mother had bought it for him two years ago, before she started worrying—and harping. Wayne had worn it to a Halloween party that year, and had won second prize (losing out to an oversized turkey). He had to hide it now, because in the middle of one of her rages last summer, his mother had thrown it out. Wayne had been lucky to rescue it. If he hadn't noticed a black sleeve poking out from under a garbage can lid, his prize-winning suit would've ended up in the landfill.

He shifted off the bed now and peered out the attic's single window, a smeary oval in the dormer overlooking the street. Outside was a dismal, drizzly Saturday, airless and unseasonably hot. And the attic always managed to be five or six degrees hotter than ambient.

There had been a huge argument over Wayne using the attic as a bedroom. His mother had taken the stance that it was unhealthy up there, too hot in summer, too damp and cold in winter. But for once his dad had taken his side and Wayne had won. He didn't mind the heat, not really, although today it was nigh on insufferable. Up here, he didn't have to be bored on a rainy Saturday. Up here he had his privacy. And to him, that was of primo importance.

"Wayne?" His mother, trumpeting from the kitchen.

He went to the attic door and hollered, "*What?*"

"I'm heading over to your Aunt Bee's for a spell. I'll be home for supper. You can fix yourself a sandwich for lunch, okay?"

It was okay with Wayne.

He scratched a pimple on his forehead. His finger came away bloody. He went back to the window and watched his mother's two-tone Pinto back out of the driveway. Then he went to the closet, dug out the SS uniform and pulled it on. He had trouble doing up the buttons on the jacket, his well-stoked belly and broadening shoulders straining at the fabric. He had to leave the top button undone, so he attached the Iron Cross under his chin to hide the defect.

Then he returned to the window and stared at the slow progression of the day, his considerable imagination playing out different scenarios of life in the Nazi regime. All that unchecked power. Imposing, blue-eyed men in uniform, taking whatever they wanted with impunity. At one point, he thought he could hear the menacing rumble of Panzers, but it was only a distant roll of thunder.

At 9:30 on that dreary morning, Jerky Jerry Jankowski pedaled by the house on his knobby-wheeled dirt bike. Jerky Jerry was . . . well, something of a birdbrain, but he was better than nobody on a day like today. Normally on summer break, Wayne would've been hanging out with the other three members of his gang, but they'd all gone out of town this morning to play against the New Liskeard Little League team. Wayne would've been with them, but his throwing wrist was still taped-up from a recent injury. As the team's star pitcher, he hated tagging along when he wasn't playing.

He cranked the window open now and hollered, "Hey, Jerk . . . uh, Jerry!" and the kid nearly toppled off his bike. He looked up, saw Wayne, and a big admiring grin split his face. Wayne said, "Hey, Jer, wait up." He closed the window, grabbed his rain slicker and dashed into the stairwell. He had an idea, something to help pass the time. It'd start with Jerry's 'initiation' into the gang: The Azilda Manglers.

He left the house by the back door and pushed his bike out to the street.

~

Jerry said, "Hi, Wayne! Boy, was I surprised when you called down to me. I nearly fell offa my bike. I'm goin' to get my dad some cigarettes . . . hey, where'd ya get the neat black suit?"

Jerry was excited. Jerry was *always* excited. His left eye was swollen almost shut with a nice purple shiner. When Jerry's dad got drunk, which was regularly, he used his son as a punching bag. Big ol' Stan Jankowski was the town's ranking tosspot.

Wayne straddled his bike now and zipped up his slicker, hiding most of the uniform, then foot-rolled the bike next to Jerry's and draped an arm around the kid's bony shoulders, saying, "Jerry, I been thinking. How'd you like to join up? Become an honorary member of the Azilda Manglers?"

Jerry lit up like a jukebox. A word caught in his throat, and for a moment he barked like a trained seal. Wayne wondered if he'd have to perform the Heimlich maneuver on the little guy.

Finally, Jerry blurted, "Yuh . . . yuh . . . yuh really mean it?" and Wayne nodded. "Wow dolly, you *bet.*"

Wayne had trouble disguising a smirk. This was going to be fun. He glanced at Jerry's twisted left hand, then looked away in disgust. Wayne's mother had explained that Jerry had been born with cerebral palsy, some kind of damage sustained during the trip out. To use his left hand—which dangled at the end of an arm that was shorter and scrawnier than normal—he had to spread the fingers with his right hand and wrap them around whatever it was he wanted to grasp. Like his handlebars. In the contracted palm of his left hand he always kept his 'dolly', a tiny plastic doll, skin-toned and naked, with teensy splayed arms and legs. Its head was bald, and the crude features of its face had been worn away by Jerry's constant rubbing. The whole thing was about the length of a book match. Wayne had asked him about it once, where he'd got it and why he carried it around all the time, but Jerry had gone eerily mute and stood staring at his sneakers. Wayne thought the creepy little nubbin might be the kid's only companion.

Jerry's expression darkened now, his excitement fading, something else creeping in. Wayne thought it was fear. Jerry said, "I gotta get my dad's cigarettes first, two decks of Player's mild. Can I join up after that?"

Wayne thought, *Let's see how bad he wants in.* He knew what'd happen to the kid if he was late with his old man's fags. "It's gotta be now, chum. Now or never. As president of the Manglers, it's up to me to make this kinda decision. The other members are in New Liskeard for the day, but I know they'll abide by my ruling."

Jerry's face twisted into a perplexed knot . . . but some of the fear was leaking out of it now, replaced by a growing defiance.

"Think long and hard, Jerry my boy. Long and hard." Wayne glanced at his watch. "I'll give you ten seconds."

Now the kid grinned and said, "Okay, I'll *do* it. I'll for sure do it. Nobody messes with the Manglers, right, Wayne?"

"That's *right.* Not even dads. Now come on. Let's head over to the office and get this done."

~

Gang headquarters—the office—was located a half-mile east of town, smack dab in the middle of the municipal dump. The only drawback to the use of the place was the caretaker, Cleo Gauthier. Next to Jerry's dad, Cleo was both literally and figuratively the biggest boozer in town, six-foot-six, three hundred and eighty pounds of mean, foul-tempered, kid-hating blubber. He kept a pellet rifle in the shack, and as every kid who'd ever trespassed at the dump and run into Cleo knew, he wasn't afraid to use it.

The boys pulled to a stop in a puddle at the entrance to the dump, a rusted Frost gate padlocked with a chain slack enough to allow brave lads like the Manglers easy access to the wonderland inside. There were deep tire runnels in the mud, but none that looked fresh.

Jerry started to say, "Is this where the office is—?" but Wayne cut him short with a finger pressed to his lips.

"*Quiet*, man." He got off his bike and leaned it against the gate. "Hide the bikes in the bushes over there. I'm gonna go on ahead, see if that fat shit Cleo's here. When you hear me whistle, come running. Stay to the left of the fork up there. I'll find you."

Jerry looked down at his hands, puzzled. Wayne tapped the left one. The twisted one. "That's your left, Jerky."

Jerry's gaze darkened, and Wayne took an uncertain step back. "When I'm in the club, no more Jerky Jerry, okay?"

Wayne nodded, then ranged ahead.

Cleo's car, a battered '63 Chevy Impala, was nowhere to be seen, and his sagging shack was abandoned. Wayne whistle loud enough to roust a flock of rummaging gulls. After a minute, looking lost and scared, Jerry appeared.

"Over here," Wayne called, and the mutt came stumbling toward him through the muck. Taking the lead now, Wayne said, "Follow me."

They stopped next to the gutted carcass of a big '53 Buick Supreme, Mangler headquarters. Prior to becoming the town dump, the six-acre yard had belonged to an ailing wrecking concern run by Archie Macauley, another model citizen. The town took it over after Archie's German Shepherd turned mean one night and did some mangling of its own. Archie never used his hands again. The town didn't bother hauling the wrecks away, some of which dated back to the '20s. The gang had chosen the Buick because it was the largest, the farthest from Cleo's shack, and had the readiest escape access.

Wayne yanked open the passenger door and the two boys crawled inside.

Jerry's eyes gleamed. "Who'da guessed? This is some neat, Wayne-o. Shit on a stick. I'm in. I'm *in*."

"Whoa, now," Wayne said, "not so fast, big fella. Two things we gotta deal with first. Number one, the membership fee. And number two—he slapped his hands together and Jerry jumped, bonking his head on the roof of the car. "Your initiation."

"Ini . . ." Jerry tried to mimic. "And a fee?"

"Well, yeah. What did you think? You'd get in for free?" He unzipped his slicker, revealing the polished brass buttons of the SS uniform. And when he spoke, he affected a German accent. "Two bucks, Queen's currency. No exceptions."

Jerry's face was a blank. Then it dawned. "You mean the cigarette money?" Wayne nodded. "No, no, no *way*." Jerry started to get up and rapped his head again, harder this time, then sat back down, dazed. "I can't do that. My dad'll break my ass. That's what he said: 'You lose that dough, meathead, I'll break your ass.'"

Wayne was silent a moment now, afraid he'd gone too far. Then he said, "Look, sweat thee not. I'll give you the weekend special. One buck, and after the initiation, I'll keep crabby old Miss O'Neill busy at the store while you scoff the cigarettes for your old man, okay?"

Jerry considered this a moment, then pulled a wadded dollar bill out of his pocket and handed it over. Wayne made it disappear, saying, "Now for the most important part. Your initiation."

Until he glanced out the narrow rear window of the Buick and saw the old Frigidaire leaning atop a pile of Azilda refuse, Wayne had no idea what he'd do with this chump. But the white enamel cubicle put him in mind of the quote he'd read earlier that morning, Dr. Mengele's observations on isolation and sensory deprivation—and he knew exactly how he'd complete this mock initiation.

"Initiation is a kind of proving ground," he said now, mimicking his dad's heart-to-heart tone. "With the initiation, a new member gets a chance to show his courage and reliability. And he also gets to show how much he trusts the other guys. See?" Jerry nodded, but his blue eyes remained merrily vacant. "Now, are you in or not?"

"You bet!"

"Okay. This way, plebe." He led the kid to the Frigidaire. The door was wide open, and Wayne yanked out two rusted metal shelves and tossed them aside. Now he stood back, and with a sweeping motion of his hand, said, "Get in."

Jerry hesitated. "You mean . . . get *in*?"

Wayne's grin broadened. "Remember what I said? Courage, reliability, and trust." He was using the German accent again, thicker now. "Get in."

Like a wary puppy, Jerry got inside. He sat with his back to the rear wall, head hung, knees drawn up to his chest. Without looking at Wayne, he plucked the dolly out of his left hand and rubbed it against his cheek.

Wayne closed the door.

"How long," he heard Jerry say, as if from a distant room.

"Till I let you out. Any screaming or fussing, you're out of the club."

That was when he saw Cleo Gauthier's car pull up to the shack.

Without hesitation, he turned tail and ran. As he lifted a strand of barbed wire in a sagging section of the back fence, he thought he heard a dull, rhythmic thumping coming from the direction of the old Frigidaire.

"How long is dad gone for this time, mom?" Wayne asked without much interest. With one eye on *M*A*S*H*, he was working his way through his favorite dinner: Shake 'n Bake chicken, Green Giant Cream Style Corn Niblets, and oven-browned potatoes. He'd changed into T-shirt and shorts, his uniform back in its hiding place behind a loose board in the attic closet.

"Seven or eight days, hon," his mother said. Wayne's father drove transport for Inco, the big international nickel company based in nearby Sudbury. He'd left for B.C. the morning before.

Wayne grinned. He liked it when his dad took off on long trips. It allowed him freer rein.

The phone rang now. Wayne glanced at his mother as she scooped up the receiver and said hello, curious about the abrupt change in her expression, her eyebrows going up as if in shock or surprise. Just as suddenly, that expression tightened into something Wayne understood all too well—concern.

She said, "Just a sec, Mister Jankowski, I'll ask my son."

Wayne's fork dropped from his hand.

His mom covered the mouthpiece and said, "Wayne, it's Jerry's dad. He sounds drunk and mad as hell. He said he sent Jerry on an errand hours ago and he hasn't come back yet. Have you seen him?"

Wayne shook his head, grunting through a mouthful of corn. He had to stifle a laugh. He'd forgotten all about poor ol' Jerky Jerry. On his way home from the dump he'd run into Stephanie Venne. Stephanie was fifteen and had enormous boobs—and a pretty solid rep for letting boys fondle them. She'd been particularly fascinated by his uniform. Not enough to allow him a squeeze on one of those yummy orbs, but she'd taken his mind completely off Jerry and his unintentionally prolonged initiation. Well, after *M*A*S*H*, he'd scoot back to the dump and let the little guy out.

Wayne's mother sympathized with Andy Jankowski for a minute, then hung up and went back to her ironing.

After *M*A*S*H* there was *All In The Family*, and after that, the dishes. After the dishes, Ryan Slater dropped by to tell Wayne about the game in New Liskeard. The Azilda Red Sox had taken a serious drubbing. It was dusk before he thought about Jerry again, pushing dark by the time he got to the dump.

Cleo's car was still parked by the shack, which at this time of day meant only one thing: Cleo was boozing, and he wasn't alone. He'd gone into Sudbury with his paycheck and picked up a hooker.

Wayne left his bike by the back fence. He winced each time his Wellingtons squelched in the mud. He kept thinking about the business end of Cleo's pellet gun.

He heard the muffled thumping before he got to the Frigidaire. In twilight, the dented appliance had a forbidding appearance and gave off an eerie enamel gleam, like a giant polished tooth. It stood aslant high up on the rubble, pregnant and thumping in a dull, mechanical cadence. If Wayne hadn't understood what that repetitive sound was, he might've thought the old refrigerator haunted. But it was just Jerky Jerry, wondering when his time would be up—and probably shitting himself about his old man's cigarettes.

Wayne thought there might be some fun left in this yet. He climbed up to the fridge and tapped on the door. "Hey Jerky, it's me. Wanna come out now?"

. . . thump . . . thump . . . thump . . .

"Hey numbnuts, your old man's on the warpath. He's gonna scalp you and hang you out for the vultures."

. . . thump . . . thump . . . thump . . .

Wayne paused, thinking back to the immortal words of Dr. Josef Mengele, Butcher of Auschwitz. He wondered if Jerry had already freaked out. Mengele's notes stated that it took the average subject several days to truly go mad, but wasn't Jerry a much less than average individual? Being a dimwit, wasn't it likely he'd lose his marbles that much sooner?

Wayne felt swollen with a sense of historical significance. Right here in Azilda, Ontario, he was continuing valuable research begun some forty years prior by members of a master race. Maybe he could send his findings in to *War Magazine*, with a Polaroid of one freaked-out Jerry Jankowski, a slobbering dodo after only eight hours of sensory deprivation. But the kid was such a dork, probably no one would notice a difference in him anyway.

. . . thump . . . thump . . .

The thumping was getting under Wayne's skin. He shuddered involuntarily, saying, "Hey Jer, why won't you talk to me? You have to say 'pretty please' before I let you out. Don't forget, Player's mild, two decks, or you'll be walking around with a broken ass for the rest of your days."

The thumping continued, but more softly now, and at a slower cadence.

"Come on, meatball," Wayne said, crouching now with an ear to the cool enamel door. "Ask me nicely or I'm fuckin' off. I mean it, dick-breath."

... thump ... thump ...

Jerry's stubborn silence sent an unexpected chill through Wayne and he said, "Okay, moron. I'll let you out if you give me that other dollar."

.... thump ....

Worried now, he tugged on the door handle. It broke off in his hand.

.... thump—

A furious female voice cut through the air; it came from Cleo's shack. "No way, you pervy son of a *bitch*. You couldn't *pay* me enough to do that. Jesus, what is *wrong* with you?"

Wayne swung around, almost tumbling from his perch in front of the fridge. A half-naked female, almost as massive as Cleo, was stomping barefoot through the sludge now, veering away from the shack, screaming obscenities. Cleo came weaving out after her, slipping and falling to his knees, making a sound like a rhino settling in for a mud bath.

"Hey, you fat cow. You still owe me fifty bucks' worth. I'll—"

That was when Cleo spotted Wayne's crouching form, silhouetted against the dimming blush of the horizon. There was only one thing Cleo hated more than recalcitrant whores, and that was sneaky, snot-nosed, trespassing kids. He lurched back into the shack, grabbed the pellet rifle, then came plodding toward the Frigidaire in his befouled Jockeys, hooting like a war-crazed Injun.

"Hey, you little bastard. Stay right where you are, boy. Uncle Cleo's gonna pepper your peepin'-Tom ass for ya! Oh, yeah, you got *that* right."

Wayne tossed the door handle into the refuse and ran like hell.

What followed was a police investigation, and a week of the hottest July weather in the history of the region. By the end of that week, police had given up on finding young Jerry Jankowski alive. One official harbored the belief the kid's old man had popped him a little too hard one night, and had called the boy in as missing in an attempt to cover his own guilty ass. That official was keeping a keen eye on Andy Jankowski, but all he was seeing was a curiously remorseful drunk who appeared to be drying out.

Investigators came around to the homes of all the kids who knew Jerry, including Wayne, who kept his lip buttoned. He'd snuck back to the dump early Sunday morning to find Cleo passed out in the front seat of the Chevy, the Frigidaire standing just as it had been the night before, minus the thumping. Guessing Jerry had found his own way out—the possibility the kid might've died in there didn't occur to him until the cops came calling a couple of days later—he'd gone back home and forgotten about the whole thing.

As the week wore on, his fears the police might find Jerry dead began to fade, and he came up with his own theory about what happened to the poor dope. In all probability, Jerry's old man had administered one too many shit kickings to the giddy mutt, and Jerry had packed up his *Beatles* knapsack, jumped on his dirt bike and run away. It seemed as good an explanation as any.

Until the phone rang one morning—a week almost to the hour after Wayne had called down to the kid from the attic window—and Ryan Slater's excited voice came bubbling over the wire. Ryan's dad was the county coroner. As Ryan spoke, Wayne's heart crept into his throat.

"Meet me at the dump, man. Sneak in the back way. My dad just got a call. I think they found Jerry. Hurry! We gotta *see* this. Sounds like it's pretty gruesome."

Sick with dread, Wayne grabbed his bike and pedaled out to the dump.

Cleo had found Jerry's bike in the brush by the front gate. Then he'd noticed a terrible stink in the vicinity of the Frigidaire, which, considering Cleo and what he was accustomed to, must've been a foul stench indeed. He busted a hole in the door with a 10-pound sledge, then alerted the authorities. They had notified Dr. Slater.

Ryan and Wayne arrived in the cover of the Buick just in time to see the fridge door pried open. The smell reached them instantly, thick, putrescent, gagging in its intensity. Two of the cops threw up on the spot. Everyone else, including Ryan's dad, turned a noticeable shade of green. Even two hundred feet away, Ryan released a strangled cough that sounded like he might puke.

In the intense July heat, the temperature in the Frigidaire must have reached broiling levels. Fascinated, Wayne thought of the ovens at Auschwitz. Jerry was shriveled, almost unrecognizable. His arms, now fleshless stakes, were extended, both hands twisted into talons. It appeared he'd been trying to claw his way out; there were blood-stained scratches on the inside of the door. What was left of his skin was blackened, pocked with runny blisters. His eyes were missing. As the boys watched, a huge black beetle crawled out of one of the sockets, and now Ryan did puke.

As they lifted the carcass into an aluminum casket, Wayne thought he saw Jerry's dolly, embedded in the bare-boned palm of his left hand.

Wayne waited until everyone left, even dirty old Cleo. Then he went looking for the door handle. He found it without any trouble. He picked it up and wiped it clean on his shirttail, then tossed it away again.

That stink followed him all the way home.

~

The feature story in the Sudbury Star explained that Jerry Jankowski, a thirteen-year-old Azilda boy, had accidentally locked himself inside a discarded refrigerator, and had suffocated to death. Once again, patrons of the dump were implored to remove the door, or at least the locking mechanism, before disposing of similar appliances.

That night, the heat in the attic was sweltering. Wayne lay naked on his single bed, trying to imagine what it must've been like for Jerry inside that fridge.

After a while, he drifted into a restless, image-filled slumber.

In the dream, he stood before the Frigidaire in twilight with the broken door handle in his grip. The hole Cleo had made with the sledge was there, and the smell issuing from it was horrible. Wayne thought he could see eyes peering out through that hole, smoldering obsidian orbs, like coals, baking with a hateful fury. Now a mouth appeared in the gap, rotted teeth bared in a lipless rictus. And a voice, felt more than heard, crisp, crackling, a jet of sooty smoke punctuating each hell-sent syllable.

"Time for your initiation, Wayne-o."

A claw blurred out through the hole and caught him by the collar.

The door began to open . . .

Wayne's eyes unblinkered in the festering heat of the attic. He was up on his elbows, a scream flexing behind his teeth like a bronco at the starting gate. From somewhere around him came a dull, thumping sound.

When he tried to move off the bed, he realized his elbows had sunk six inches into the substance of the mattress.

He lurched to his feet with a startled shout, rapping his skull against the slanted roof of the attic. He grabbed each of his elbows in turn. They were fine. Now he stared at the mattress. Normal. No sinkholes.

Damn, he thought, *what a freaky dream. No way I'm getting back in that bed.*

He pulled on his shorts and padded down to the second floor. As quietly as he was able, he slipped into his parents' bedroom and crawled in beside his mother's sleeping form.

She stirred. "What are you doing here?"

"Bad dream."

"Well, you listen to me, Wayne Lamoreaux, you're a big boy now. You need to trot right back up to your room this instant. Your father would never allow—"

"Please, Ma . . . I was out at the dump today. I saw . . ."

"Oh," she said, and touched his face. "All right then. But just for tonight. Your dad'll be home tomorrow, anyway." She turned her back to him now and went back to sleep.

Although he tried, Wayne didn't sleep another wink.

For the next two nights, he bunked in on the living room couch. His mother saw this is a way of getting him out of the attic and back into the spare bedroom; in anticipation, she began preparing the room. His father saw it as a cowardly streak, and on the third night ordered him back up to the attic.

Wayne stared at the bed for a long time before getting onto it, and even then he only sat on the edge, running a palm over its surface. It was quite late before he lay down, and even though he was exhausted, he had a tough time nodding off. His senses were like a fresh wound. Shortly after midnight, the fatigue claimed him. The dream came instantly, as it had that first night.

There was the Frigidaire, angled into the trash, thumping out its lunatic beat. And that smell, like marooned jellyfish rotting in sunbaked tide pools. And beyond the hole Cleo had made, those glinting, lifeless eyes, that lipless maw.

The fridge door hissed open. The thing behind it stepped out.

"Got my own gang now, Wayne-o. Wanna join?"

Now it caught him by the throat and shoved him into the fridge. Unassisted, the door slammed tight to its frame.

Terrified, Wayne peered through the hammer hole.

It was Jerky Jerry out there alright, or whatever was left of him. Empty sockets for eyes, wads of broiled flesh hanging from bleached bones gleaming in the moonlight.

"Let you out for a buck . . . weekend special . . ."

The walls of the Frigidaire began to close in.

"Better hurry . . . I'll give you ten seconds . . ."

Wayne screamed. He screamed and screamed and screamed.

Wayne's mother sat up in bed, then jabbed her husband in the ribs.

"Not tonight, baby," he muttered. "Too tired."

"I heard a scream, Terry. I think it was Wayne." She swung her legs off the bed. "Come on, I need you to come with me. Come *on*."

Terry shifted into a sitting position, rubbing his eyes. "I didn't hear nothing, Eve."

"Maybe he's having another nightmare. Come on. You're his father."

"Are you sure?"

Eve caught her husband by the wrist and together they climbed the stairs to the attic bedroom.

It was abandoned; Wayne wasn't there. They called and called, searching the house and the yard. But their son was gone.

There was still no sign of him next morning. Another police investigation was commenced. The official who'd suspected

Jerry's father now believed there was a homicidal pedophile on the loose. He had his men search the dump again, turning his attention to Cleo Gauthier now, who went right on whoring and boozing.

Terry Lamoureux took the next few days off work to help with the search. But jobs were scarce, able bodies abounded, and on Friday he was he was forced to return to his rig. Reluctantly, he set out for Winnipeg that morning. He would keep in touch with Eve by phone.

Alone in the house, Eve wallowed in a desperate melancholy. The weekend was a misery of fear, uncertainty, and growing despair. Every time the phone rang, her nerves erupted like miniature spring toys from the tin box of constant expectancy. Usually it was only well-meaning friends, calling to offer sympathy and support. Occasionally, it was one of the detectives; always they had nothing to report.

After that first night, the night Wayne went missing, she felt unable to go up to his room. Twice she went as far as the door; once, she opened it partway. Both times a stale, vacant odor from in there prevented her from going any farther.

Monday night, almost out of her mind with dread, she mounted the attic steps. It seemed her son had simply vanished. It hadn't taken a minute to get to his bedroom after hearing the screams. The attic window was latched from the inside, and beyond it was a sheer, three-story drop to the pavement. To gain access to the attic using the staircase, a kidnapper would've had to walk right past the master bedroom. She had gone through her son's closet and bureau drawers that night, and had been able to account for every stitch of clothing he owned. If someone had taken him, they'd taken him naked. She even found that godforsaken SS uniform, which she marched right down to the woodstove and torched finally and for good. She did likewise with all of those dreadful photos and other bits of Nazi crapola. And in some dark way she was unable to articulate, her gut told her that Nazi stuff was somehow connected to Wayne's disappearance.

And, although the thought punished her horribly, she knew it had something to do with the Jankowski boy's unfortunate end as well. She remembered Wayne dropping his cutlery in surprise the afternoon Andy Jankowski called looking for his son. And she had found that underlined section in Wayne's book, the one about the concentration camp.

There was still that stale smell in the attic, but it was stronger now: pungent, a whiff of death. She sat on her son's bed and ran an affectionate hand across the counterpane, wondering if she'd ever see him again. Almost unnoticed, her palm rippled over a series of small, evenly-spaced bumps in the mattress beneath the sheet.

She heard a scurrying sound now, beneath her, and when she realized what it was, the knowledge struck her like a dropkick. *Mice!* There were goddamn mice in her son's mattress! On top of everything else, this was the last straw.

An enormous spillway of loss, frustration and pain opened inside Eve Lamoreaux, a vent that released the pent-up anticipation of the past several days and converted it to rage. With murderous ferocity, she stripped off the bedding, grabbed a pair of scissors from Wayne's study table and began stabbing and ripping at the mattress.

With the first half-dozen thrusts, she reached springs and foam. A mouse appeared, squealed in terror and dashed for a rent in the padding. A low growl issued from Eve's throat as she seized the hapless rodent and jammed its furry body between the stainless-steel jaws of the scissors. There was a final squeal, alarmingly shrill for the size of the creature, and a spurt of warm blood.

Then Eve was hacking at the mattress again, ripping, gouging, grunting with fury. With one raging pull, she tore back a huge section of fabric, revealing more springs and foam padding, dozens of scrambling mice, and her son's decomposing corpse.

His hair was no longer that Aryan, platinum blond; it was a matted yellow now, like moldy straw. His clear blue eyes were gone. His hands were claws at the ends of partially extended arms;

it seemed he'd been trying to dig his way out of the mattress. It had been his fingertips Eve felt, poking up from his Posture-Pedic sarcophagus.

In his left hand was a tiny plastic doll.

Eve ran screaming from her son's room. It was a scream that would never end.

ABOUT THE AUTHOR

Sean Costello is the author of nine novels and numerous screenplays. His thriller *Here After* has been optioned to film by David Hackl, director of *Saw V*. Sean's horror novels have drawn comparisons to the works of Stephen King, his thrillers to those of Elmore Leonard. All of his titles are currently available as ebooks, wherever ebooks are sold.

If you enjoyed *Miscreations*, check out *Here After*.

Reviews are the lifeblood of indie authors. If you enjoyed this collection, please consider leaving a review on whichever retail platform you use.

www.ingramcontent.com/pod-product-compliance
Lightning Source LLC
LaVergne TN
LVHW051018080826
845145LV00009B/2689

* 9 7 8 1 9 9 8 3 3 1 5 1 2 *